Chapter One

$\mathcal{M}$aud Montague looked around the bedroom she shared with her twin sister Milly. The room was divided into two very different halves. Maud's half had jet-black wallpaper, and was so cluttered you couldn't see the carpet. Beneath Maud's bed was her pet rat Quentin's daytime den, made of old twigs and bits of cardboard box.

"You're such a messy-potamus," said Milly. "No wonder you can never find anything!"

Milly's half had soppy pink wallpaper. She'd packed all her things away in her lilac chest of drawers, except for her teddy bears and dolls, which she'd lined up on top in order of size.

"I tidied up once and I was looking for stuff for weeks," said Maud. "This way, I know exactly where everything is."

Milly buttoned her creaseless, navy blue blazer in front of her full-length mirror. "Perfect," she said. "Now for yummy porridge." She ran downstairs, singing to herself.

Maud followed her sister downstairs, passing the family portraits and waving at the one of her favourite ancestor, Great-aunt Ethel. She opened the dining-room door, sat down between her mum and dad, and selected a piece of toast from the metal rack.

Mr Montague was examining a car's exhaust pipe, and leaving an oily stain on the white tablecloth.

His wife was carefully checking through a box of rubber bats she'd bought for the upcoming performance of *Dracula* at their local theatre. She was in charge of props and costumes.

"Are you looking forward to your sleepover on Saturday, Milly?" asked Mr Montague.

Milly's sleepover! Maud had completely forgotten about it. She had told her parents she'd ask some friends along too, but now she wasn't so sure. Maud's friends were quite … unusual. She didn't think they would get on with Milly.

"It's going to be brillingtons," said Milly. "Poppy Simpkins is coming, and Alice Jones and Suzie Singh, and we're going to learn the new dance routine by the Sparkle Club Girls. They're my favourite band of all time. We can teach you, too, if you like, Maud."

Maud was just swallowing a mouthful of toast as Milly said this, but she managed to keep it down.

"Have you invited anyone, Maud?" asked Mrs Montague.

Maud didn't really want to ask anyone to the sleepover, because Maud had a secret. While Milly went to Primrose Towers – a prim girls' school – Maud went to a school for vampires, werewolves, ghosts, witches and other monsters. Even though Maud's great-aunt Ethel was the head teacher, she was a ghost herself. Nobody else in the family knew Rotwood wasn't an ordinary school. If Milly met Maud's monster friends, it would be difficult to stop her family finding out.

"Of course she hasn't," said Milly, licking her porridgey lips. "Maud hasn't got any friends."

"Actually I've got plenty," said Maud.

"It's just a shame these so-called friends are all busy on Saturday," snorted Milly.

"Well, that's where you're wrong," said Maud. "Because I've already asked … er … two of them to come along. And they've both agreed."

"Well, that sounds like it will be fun for everyone," said Mrs Montague. She'd just finished tying a piece of elastic to one of the fake bats, and she was flapping it up and down.

"I vont to bite your neck," said Mrs Montague. "Mwa ha ha!"

Maud was tempted to tell her mum that vampires didn't really talk like that. And she should know – there were several at Rotwood.

"Tooth time!" announced Milly and she darted upstairs. Milly brushed her teeth three times every morning, first with mint-flavoured paste, then with baking soda and then with a lemon and herb mixture.

"Isn't your *Dracula* performance on Saturday night?" Maud asked her mum.

"That's right, petal," said Mrs Montague, "and Tracy's babysitting."

"Maybe I could help with that instead of staying here for the sleepover," said Maud.

"Oh no," said Maud's mum. "I'll be running around looking after the props, and your dad will be up in the lighting box, so there won't be anyone to keep an eye on you."

"I won't need anyone to keep an eye on me," said Maud.

Mr Montague raised an eyebrow. "You said that about your sister's ballet recital."

When Maud had gone to her sister's ballet performance, her pet rat had escaped on to the stage and caused havoc.

"But I won't bring Quentin this time," said Maud. "It would be far too scary for him."

"It's too late now anyway," said Mrs Montague. "You've already invited your friends to the sleepover."

"I suppose so," said Maud, and she nipped off to the garage to check on Quentin. On the way, she grabbed a carton of milk and a packet of crisps so she could top up his supplies. He squeaked with delight as she emptied the crisps into his bowl.

"What am I going to do, Quentin?" asked Maud. "I've promised to bring a couple of friends from school along, and I haven't got a clue who to invite." She watched Quentin tuck into the snacks, blissfully ignoring her. "If those Primrose Towers girls thought you were fearsome," Maud muttered, "wait until they meet the monsters from Rotwood."

Chapter Two

Maud was sitting in the cavernous assembly hall of Rotwood School, while the pupils sang their morning hymns.

All things dark and horrible,
All creatures cruel and sly,
All things dim and terrible,
That love to make kids cry …

She looked at her friends. Who on earth could she invite to the sleepover without the Primrose Towers girls discovering her monster secret?

Sitting to Maud's left was Paprika, who was

half vampire and half human. He had pale white skin, slicked-back hair and a long black cape, but could just about pass for human – as long as he didn't smile and show off his fangs. Even better, Paprika was the only student at Rotwood who knew that Maud was a human girl and only pretending to be a monster.

Sitting to Maud's right was Wilf, a werewolf with thick brown hair covering his face and hands. It would be more difficult to convince her family that he was normal. Maybe she could wrap him in bandages and pretend he'd been in an accident. The same went for Martin the mummy – and at least he came already wrapped.

Sitting next to Wilf was Zombie Zak, who had rotting grey skin and glassy, sunken eyes. Maud didn't think she could invite him. His arm might drop off halfway through a dance routine.

Poisonous Penelope was sitting at the end.

She was a witch with straggly purple hair, wearing a pointed black hat. She looked a lot more human than most of the Rotwood pupils, but Maud didn't think it would be a good idea to invite her. She'd only spend the whole time looking for new ways to be horrible to everyone.

But she had to invite someone, because her family were expecting her to.

When the hymn had finished, all the pupils sat down on the hard wooden pews. The Head of Rotwood – Maud's great-aunt Ethel – walked through the lectern at the front of the hall.

"Mr Quasimodo the caretaker will be taking next week off in light of his recent workload," said the Head. She adjusted her large round glasses and glared at Maud.

Maud shrank down in her pew, blushing with shame. A couple of weeks ago, she'd left the door to the school greenhouse open, making Venus flytraps grow over the playing fields. It had taken the poor caretaker ages to chop them all down.

"While Mr Quasimodo's away," continued the Head, "I'll need someone to look after his pet hamster, Violet. Any volunteers?"

Cries of horror echoed around the hall.

"Who would want that thing in their house?" asked Oscar, the boy with a detachable head.

"I could never sleep with something like *that* watching me," said Bart Bones, a skeleton sitting next to him.

Hardly a surprise, thought Maud. Rotwood pupils hated anything cute or cuddly. Furry rodents were as terrifying to them as snakes and spiders were to humans.

"Come on now," said the Head. "There must be someone …"

Maud felt her right arm tingle. It shot up into the air as if yanked by an invisible string.

"Excellent, Maud," said the Head. "It's so wonderful to see someone willing to take responsibility."

Maud tried to pull her right arm down with her left, but it was no use. It was stuck in the air. She heard a faint muttering from the back of the hall and turned around to see Poisonous Penelope holding her hands out and mouthing a spell.

As soon as Penelope saw she'd been spotted, she stopped, and Maud's arm fell back down again. Maud looked at the front of the hall, ignoring Penelope. She didn't want to give her the satisfaction of seeing her angry.

✳ ✦ ✳ ☆ ★ ✳ ✦

After they'd sung 'Give Me Gloom in my Heart', the pupils filed out of the assembly hall to their morning lessons. Maud caught up with Wilf and Paprika.

"What are you guys doing on Saturday night?" she asked.

"My parents are going out," said Paprika. "So Grandpa's coming round to look after me. I'm not looking forward to it, though. He insists that I sleep in a coffin in the basement. He's so old-fashioned."

"I'm going to play *Fetch 2: Return of the Stick*," said Wilf. "It's totally addictive. Why?"

"I was wondering if you'd like to come to a sleepover at my house instead," said Maud.

"Count me in," said Wilf. "That sounds monstrous!"

"Me too," said Paprika. "We can cancel Grandpa, and I won't have to listen to any of his boring stories about the eighteenth century."

"Thanks, I'd love to," said a voice from next to him. "I'm so glad someone remembered me for once."

The voice belonged to Invisible Isabel. It would be mean to say she couldn't come now.

At least Isabel wouldn't scare the Primrose Towers girls. They wouldn't even know she was there.

Maud was just about to go upstairs to her classroom, when Mr Quasimodo opened the door to his office and beckoned her in with a grunt.

The office was one of the few places Maud had seen that was even messier than her half of the bedroom. The entire floor was covered with empty paint pots, squashed tubes of glue and broken mops. Maud found it strange that a man who was meant to keep an entire school tidy couldn't even look after his own office.

"You take care," said Mr Quasimodo, thrusting a metal cage at Maud. Inside the cage was a hamster with pure white fur. It was sitting perfectly still at the bottom of the cage, staring up at Maud with vivid violet eyes.

"Read instructions," he said, handing Maud a scrap of paper that had been ripped from a notepad.

"Thanks," said Maud. "I hope you enjoy your holiday. Where are you going, by the way? On a tour of Victorian graveyards? A trip to a castle in Transylvania? Or are you bell-ringing in Paris again?"

"Costa Del Sol," said Mr Quasimodo. "Fun and sun."

He ushered her out of the office and slammed the door. Unfortunately, this made the scrap of paper blow out of Maud's hand. She tried to run after it, but it fluttered out of the window.

Maud heard a snigger behind her in the corridor and turned to see a flash of purple hair disappearing around the corner. Penelope?

Oh well. Maud didn't need the instructions anyway. She knew plenty about looking after rodents, thanks to Quentin.

But as she made her way down the corridor, Maud began to wonder: it was rather odd that Mr Quasimodo had needed to write a full page of notes.

How hard could it be to care for a hamster?

Chapter Three

It was early Saturday evening, and Maud's mum was looking for her scissors. She was preparing for the opening night of the *Dracula* musical.

"Found them!" said Mrs Montague. "Now where did I put my needle and thread?"

"You're holding them," said Maud.

"This is going to be a disaster," said Mrs Montague, chopping a strip of material from the back of a costume.

"I'm sure it will be fine," said Mr Montague.

Maud wasn't sure, though. She had almost

snorted out her orange juice when she'd found out that the actress playing the damsel in distress was Miss Bloom, her old teacher from Primrose Towers. Maud remembered her lank brown hair and lilac cardigan. She couldn't think of anyone less likely to stand on a moonlit veranda in a ballgown while a vampire chomped into her neck.

"No, it won't," said Mrs Montague. "The dress is all wrong ..."

Just then, Milly flounced into the living room and shouted, "Hurrah! It's sleepover Saturday!"

Milly broke into her Sparkle Club Girls dance routine, which involved spinning around and juddering as if she was being electrocuted.

"You girls must promise to be good for the babysitter tonight," said Mrs Montague, frantically stitching.

Maud and Milly groaned together. Maud didn't agree with her sister on much, but they both disliked Tracy. She was a sixteen-year-old from across the street, whose idea of babysitting was to stare at the TV screen, pausing only to shout at them if they made the slightest bit of noise.

The doorbell rang, and Milly darted off to answer it. A few moments later, she skipped back in, followed by her friends Poppy, Alice and Suzie.

"Thanks for having us, Mr and Mrs Montague," they chimed in perfect harmony.

Maud sighed. It was going to be a long night.

"Hello, Maud," said Poppy. "Are you enjoying your new school?"

"It's alright," said Maud. She wanted to say that it was brilliant and that Fright Classes were the best lessons ever, but she didn't want to give too much away. "How's Primrose Towers?"

"Much quieter since you left," said Poppy.

They were interrupted by a loud thumping on the roof.

"Ow!" shouted a voice from outside. Maud dashed out into the garden and found Paprika lying face down, with his cape rumpled over the back of his head.

"What happened?" asked Maud.

"Mum wouldn't give me money for the bus," said Paprika, getting up and smoothing his hair down. "She told me to fly. But next door's chimney got in the way."

Maud ushered him inside and into the living room. "Everyone, this is Paprika," she said.

"Hello, Paprika," said Mr Montague. "That's an unusual name. Is it Polish?"

"Maybe," said Paprika. "My mum's family is from Transylvania. That's near Poland, isn't it?"

"Excuse me," said Milly, narrowing her eyes at Paprika. "No boys allowed at sleepovers. It's against the rules."

"What rules?" said Maud.

Milly folded her arms and looked over to their mum, but Mrs Montague just said, "You mustn't be unpleasant to Maud's friends, dear."

"Talking of friends, I forgot to tell you that Wilf can't come," said Mr Montague. "His parents called to say that he's going out with his family tonight."

Maud glanced out of the window, where the autumn sky was already darkening. It seemed like a strange time for a family outing.

"It's going to be a full moon tonight," whispered Paprika. "Werewolves always have family gatherings on full moons. It's tradition. Like when humans have barbecues on rainy bank holidays."

"Only one friend, Maud?" said Suzie. "I suppose that is an improvement."

"Don't worry about it," said Mr Montague.

"I've invited that other nice friend of yours instead."

"Which nice friend?" asked Maud. Her mum had only ever met Penelope, but there was nothing nice about *her*.

The doorbell chimed again. Maud answered it to find Penelope standing there with a sly grin on her face. She'd taken off her pointed hat and brushed her purple hair into a neat centre parting.

Penelope pushed past into the living room, and Maud tried to close the door. It seemed to be stuck, so she gave it a firmer shove.

"Ouch," said a voice. "Watch out!"

"Oh hello, Isabel," said Maud. "Come in."

This was going to be interesting.

$$\times \; \star \; \times \; \star \; \times \; \star \;$$

"A few house rules," said Mrs Montague. "Make sure you're in bed by nine. Be nice and polite to Tracy. Don't make too much noise and don't leave the house under any circumstances. Is that understood?"

"Yes, Mrs Montague," said the Primrose Towers girls.

"Yes, Mrs Montague," said Penelope, smiling sweetly. She kept glancing around the living room at the framed family photographs. Penelope had come around to the house a couple of weeks before, and ever since then she'd been trying to force Maud to admit she wasn't a real monster. No doubt she'd agreed to come to the sleepover so she could investigate further.

"Can we try out my new baking set?" asked Milly.

"Alright," said Mrs Montague. "But don't make too much mess." She looked down at her watch and paced off into the living room.

"Can we make scrummy cupcakes?" asked Suzie.

"Yes," said Alice. "Let's have a bake-off!

Primrose Towers versus Rotwood. If they're up to it, that is."

"Maud couldn't even make a cheese sandwich," said Milly.

"Let's do it!" said Penelope.

Maud sighed. The only thing they'd ever been taught to cook at Rotwood was maggot soup.

Milly opened her baking set, which was a huge pink container with hearts on the side. Inside Maud could see measuring jugs, scales and spatulas made from the same pink plastic, and two metal baking tins with space for six cupcakes each. Milly took one out, handed it to Maud, and said, "Let the bake-off commence."

Maud grabbed a tub of margarine and a pint of milk from the fridge, while Paprika fetched packets of flour and sugar from the cupboard.

Penelope got a mixing bowl and wooden spoon out from under the sink.

Maud laid everything out on their half of the worktop. "Do we need anything else?"

"Mum uses Type A Negative blood in the cakes she makes," said Paprika. "But I don't like the taste, so I never eat them."

"You've forgotten the dead flies," said Penelope. "You can't make cupcakes without dead flies. And you'll need some crunchy spider legs to sprinkle on top."

"We're, um, out of both," said Maud. "We'll just have to make do with what we've got."

Paprika emptied out the entire packet of flour into the bowl and spooned in the margarine in large chunks. At the other end of the worktop, Poppy was carefully measuring out flour with the pink scales.

"Do you think that's enough margarine?" asked Paprika. The tub was almost empty.

"I think so," said Maud. She glanced over

at Poppy, who was pouring a teaspoon of vanilla essence into the mix.

"Who cares?" asked Penelope. "No one will eat the cakes if there are no spiders on top. That's where all the flavour comes from."

"I don't know why you came, if all you're going to do is complain," said Maud.

"If you must know, I came to see how Violet was getting on," said Penelope.

"Fine, I think," said Maud. "She's asleep in her cage."

Maud pointed to the cage in the corner of the kitchen, which she'd covered with a tea towel.

Penelope smirked.

Hmm, thought Maud. What was she up to?

After Paprika had finished pouring the ingredients into the bowl, Isabel mixed them with the wooden spoon. Maud was worried that the Primrose Towers girls would see the spoon churning around on its own, but they were distracted by their own baking.

"Mum!" shouted Milly. "We're ready for the cooker now!"

Mrs Montague came in and placed both baking trays on the middle shelf of her oven. Then she glanced down at her watch and dashed back into the living room, muttering, "Tracy ought to be here by now."

"Let's check on Violet," said Penelope, whipping the tea towel off the cage.

Maud was expecting to see Violet nestled comfortably in her straw. Instead, she was shocked to find that the hamster was actually hanging upside down from the top bars.

"Er … do hamsters do that?" asked Isabel.

Violet opened her eyes and flopped down on to the bottom of her cage. As soon as she'd done so, Poppy noticed her and barged over.

"Cute!" she squealed. "Look at her hands!"

"What's her name?" asked Alice.

"Violet," said Maud. "And they're paws, not hands."

"Hmm," said Milly. "I think she deserves a much prettier name than that."

"Let's call her Princess Snuggly," said Poppy.

"No, let's call her Fluffy," said Alice.

"No," said Milly. "I've decided that we'll call her Cuddles."

The Primrose Towers girls crowded around the hamster's cage and cooed.

"She's so sweet!"

"How adorable!"

Maud peered over their shoulders to check they weren't frightening the poor animal with their fussing. Violet seemed perfectly fine, though.

Maud heard the doorbell ring again and went into the living room to find Tracy trudging in.

The babysitter was dressed in a long black skirt and a purple t-shirt and had dark make-up around her eyes that made her look like a tired panda. She had her earphones in and was chewing gum in time with the music.

"How are you, Tracy?" asked Mr Montague.

Tracy took one of her earphones out and said, "What?"

"I was just asking how you were," said Mr Montague.

"Whatever," she said.

"We're off now," said Mrs Montague. "We'll be at the theatre if you need us. The details are on this flyer." She put a leaflet on the table and ushered her husband out.

"Bye Mum, bye Dad," said Maud, closing the front door.

"By the way, Penelope," she heard from

behind her. She turned around to see Milly giving the witch a suspicious look. "Why *is* your hair purple?"

Maud sighed. It was going to be a long night.

Chapter Four

Maud was on her way to the garage to check on Quentin, when she glanced up the stairs and noticed the portrait of her great-aunt Ethel. She'd forgotten all about the picture. The last thing she wanted was for Penelope and Paprika to find out she was related to the headmistress of Rotwood. Maud unhooked the picture, dashed upstairs and hid it in a drawer.

When she got down to the garage, she found that Quentin had burrowed deep into the sawdust at the back of his cage and was taking a nap.

"Wake up, Quentin," Maud said softly.

Quentin stretched and replied with a sleepy squeak.

Bang! Maud heard a loud noise from the kitchen and thought she'd better go and investigate. She took Quentin's cage along, so she could keep an eye on him.

Everyone had gathered to look at Tracy, who was covered in tiny pieces of pink cake.

"Oh, what a hilarious joke," Tracy said. "Give the babysitter an exploding cake."

"We didn't give it to you," said Milly. "It was you who took it out of the oven. It probably just wasn't ready yet."

Maud noticed that Penelope was stifling a giggle with her hand. Another spell, no doubt, to get them all into trouble.

"Upstairs, all of you," said Tracy. "Right now!" She glared at Quentin's and Violet's cages. "And take those disgusting vermin with you."

"That's no way to talk about Maud's friends,"

said Milly, and her Primrose Towers friends giggled.

* ✳ ★ ✩ ✱ ✦ ✳

Maud went upstairs, holding Quentin's cage. Paprika followed, carrying Violet's cage. Penelope came next, still sniggering to herself.

"We're going into the bathroom," said Milly. "No Rotwood rejects allowed."

"We don't care," said Maud. "We're going to the bedroom. No Primrose princesses allowed."

"See you three later," said Poppy.

"You four," muttered Isabel.

Maud led the way into her bedroom and sat on her bed. She scooped Quentin out of his cage to stroke him, but he wriggled out of her hands and ducked under her pillow. "Anyone for a game of Monopoly?" she asked.

"I've never heard of that," said Paprika. He was sitting on the chair in front of Milly's dressing table with Violet in his lap. "Do you have Diabolical Pursuit? Sea Serpents and Ladders? Hungry Hellhounds?"

"I don't think so," said Maud. "I've got Twister, though."

"I hate that game," said Isabel. "That's the one where everyone stands on your hands and they don't even apologise."

"I thought games like Monopoly and Twister were for humans," said Penelope, her eyes narrowing. She was examining Maud's half of the bedroom. "In fact, you seem to have a lot of human things."

"Have I?" asked Maud. "I've never really thought about it."

A chorus of giggles came from the bathroom, followed by shrill squeals.

"What are they up to?" Paprika asked.

"I don't know," said Maud.

"Well, whatever it is they're doing, they're going to have to stop," said Penelope, "because I need to use the toilet." She stomped out of the room and across to the bathroom.

"Don't worry about the noises," said Paprika to Violet, who was sitting on his lap.

Violet didn't look in the least bit nervous as she sat there, perfectly still. She looked like she could sit through an earthquake without blinking.

There was a shout from the bathroom, and Paprika's eyes widened.

"Don't touch me!" shouted Penelope again.

Paprika looked at Maud. They were both thinking the same thing. Something was making Penelope cross. They ran into the hallway as the sound of a struggle came from behind the bathroom door, and Maud heard the witch start to mutter.

"Quick, she really mustn't cast a spell,"

she whispered to Paprika. She hammered on the door. "Let Penelope out, or I'll ... I'll ..." she yelled, firmly.

Suddenly, the bolt slid across, and the bathroom door opened. Huge swirls of steam billowed out into the hallway, and Penelope ran out. As she emerged from the mist, Maud saw that her face was covered in Milly's mud mask, and her wiry purple hair had been forced into curlers.

"We're doing makeovers," Milly explained.

"I ... I ... I want to go home," said Penelope. Her hands shook as she pulled the rollers out of her hair. "I don't like this game."

Maud felt a little sorry for Penelope. She'd never exactly been fond of her, but she didn't think Penelope deserved this torture. A makeover was probably just as frightening for a witch as a night in a slime-pit would be for a human. So frightening that Penelope probably hadn't even been able to cast a spell.

✳ ✦ ✳ ★ ✩ ★ ✳ ★

"Noooo ...!" howled Milly, who was now standing in the bedroom doorway.

"What now?" asked Maud.

She ran back to the bedroom door and peered in past Milly. She couldn't believe it. In the couple of minutes she'd been away, the room had been completely trashed!

Chapter Five

*I*t looked as if a hurricane had blown through the bedroom. Maud's half looked pretty much the same, but Milly's was unrecognisable.

All the drawers had been dragged out of the dressing table and their contents were tossed randomly around. All over Milly's side of the floor, white socks and pink dresses were muddled up with dolls and her collection of Magic Dream Princess books.

"I knew this would happen," cried Milly. "I told Mum these Rotwood scruffs would vandalise the house, but she wouldn't listen."

"Was this you, Isabel?" Maud whispered.

"How could it have been?" Isabel said. "I was with you the whole time."

"If you say so."

Maud wondered if Penelope could have cast some sort of untidying spell on the room while she was in the bathroom, but it seemed unlikely. She was far too upset about her makeover to think about what was going on in the bedroom.

She noticed that her pillow was on the floor, but Quentin had disappeared.

"Has anyone seen Quentin?" she asked.

"And Violet," added Paprika. "I left her on the bed."

"Never mind about them," said Milly. "Help me pick up my stuff. I need to check nothing's broken."

Maud trod carefully across the floor, making sure she didn't accidentally step on either of the rodents. She noticed that one of Milly's white vests was quivering very slightly, and she lifted it up to discover Violet sitting casually on her back legs and rubbing her paws together. The hamster didn't flinch at all, as Maud lifted her up on to the dressing table. She was sure there was something odd about the hamster, but she couldn't quite work it out. Was it her eyes? They seemed to be glowing like lamps.

Quentin proved a little harder to find. Maud turned over all the books, monster costumes and masks on her side of the room with no luck. It was only when she looked behind her desk in the corner of the room that she found him, pressed tightly between one of the back legs of her table and the skirting board.

"What's spooked you?" Maud asked. "You look like you've seen a cat."

She carried Quentin back over to her bed, where he curled up into a ball.

"I know what will cheer your disgusting rat up," said Suzie. "Let's make him a costume."

"We could make him some beautiful fairy wings," said Alice.

"We could knit him a lovely cardigan like the one I made for my teddy bear," said Poppy.

"I've got an even better idea," said Milly. "Let's make him a wedding suit. Then he can get married to Violet."

"Oh super!" said Suzie.

"How romantic!" said Alice.

Milly grasped hold of Quentin, who struggled in her hand.

"I don't think he's very keen on the idea," said Maud.

"Nonsense," said Milly. "He's looking forward to it. Why wouldn't he be?"

"Let's get your bunny, too, Milly," squealed Poppy.

Milly shook her head. "Lollipop's been really boring ever since she got sick last week. And anyway, we'd have to go outside to the hutch to fetch her, and I don't want to."

Tracy opened the bedroom door and shoved a pizza leaflet into Maud's hand.

"I'm ordering from here," she said. "What do you lot want?"

"We'll have a Margherita," said Milly from over in the corner.

"Boring!" said Penelope, who seemed to have recovered from her ordeal already. She snatched the leaflet from Maud's hand and scanned through it. "What sort of pizza place is this? They don't even have Locust and Pineapple. I suppose it will have to be a Meat Feast."

"Don't forget, I'm vegetarian," said Paprika.

"That's okay," said Maud. "Let's get one that's half Meat Feast and half Vegetarian Delight."

"Fine," said Tracy, slamming the door.

"Ta-da!" cried Milly, holding up Quentin in his wedding costume. He had a white scarf made from a scrap of handkerchief and a black top hat made out of a marker pen lid, held on with a rubber band. His tiny pink feet were floundering up and down, desperately seeking the floor.

"And here's the beautiful bride," said Poppy, holding up Violet. She'd made her a bouquet of daisies and a tiara of tinfoil.

"Put them in the wedding carriage," said Suzie, wheeling the open-top car from Milly's old Barbie collection across the floor. Milly and Poppy plonked the rodents down in the back seat. Quentin tried to scrabble out, but he couldn't get a grip. Violet nuzzled up to him, and he struggled frantically against her, squeaking and hissing, his nose twitching wildly.

"What on earth has got into you, Quentin?" asked Maud, rescuing her rat and putting him back into his cage. She carried it back to her bed. She glanced back at Violet. The hamster's eyes were even brighter now, glowing brilliant indigo as she watched them from the toy car. Maud had always thought that hamsters were peaceful animals. Now she wasn't so sure.

Chapter Six

As soon as she heard the doorbell, Maud ran down to collect the pizzas.

"Promise you'll be quiet," said Tracy, holding the pizza boxes high above Maud's head as she jumped up for them. "There's a horror film called *Night Creepers* on TV tonight, and there's no way I'll be able to get properly frightened if I can hear you messing about."

"I promise," said Maud.

She ran upstairs with the pizza boxes and placed them in the middle of the room.

"Mum says we should always wash our

hands before we eat," said Milly. "Especially when we've been touching dirty rodents."

They all piled into the corridor to queue for the bathroom. Maud could see Poppy at the front of the queue rubbing lavender moisturiser into her hands.

"Hurry up," shouted Maud. "The pizza's going cold."

Maud was last to wash her hands. As soon as she finished, she ran back into the bedroom. But when she picked up the monsters' pizza box, it weighed practically nothing. She threw the lid back. Someone had already scoffed half the pizza! The vegetarian half was untouched, but on the other side of the box there was nothing but a slither of crust and a smear of tomato sauce.

"Who stole my half?" asked Penelope.

"Well, it wasn't me," said Paprika, scooping up a vegetarian slice. "I hate meat."

"Ours is fine, too," said Milly, biting into a slice of cheese and tomato. "Mmm, yummy."

"It must have been Isabel," said Penelope, folding her arms.

"Who's that?" asked Milly. "Aren't you a bit old for imaginary friends?"

Poppy, Alice and Suzie giggled.

"It wasn't me," muttered Isabel in Maud's ear. "I always get blamed for everything. It's not fair."

"I think it must have been Violet," said Paprika.

"Don't be ridiculous," said Milly. "Hamsters are vegetarian."

"Yeah," said Alice. "I think I'd have remembered if I'd seen one killing a gazelle on a wildlife documentary."

Maud looked over at Violet, who was now snoozing happily on the doll's house sofa with her paws resting on her round belly. Was that a scrap of pepperoni on her whiskers?

"I'm hungry," said Penelope, as Milly dangled a piece of stringy cheese into her mouth.

"I'll find us something else," said Maud.

She went downstairs to look in the fridge. There was a loaf of garlic bread in there, which was almost as good as pizza. She popped it in the microwave.

As she tiptoed past the living room, she could hear chilling stabs of violin music interrupted by screams and splatters.

✳ ✱ ✳ ✩ ★ ✳

When Maud got back to the bedroom, she found the Primrose Towers girls crowded around Milly's chest of drawers and painting their nails with glittery red nail varnish. Poppy was kneeling down beside the doll's house, dabbing some on Violet's claws.

Penelope and Paprika sat slumped on Maud's bed with their heads in their hands.

"Well, this is a great sleepover," said Penelope. "I think I'd rather be in one of Mr Von Bat's History lessons."

"I know how to liven things up," said Maud. "We could turn the lights off and tell ghost stories."

"Oh yes!" said Paprika. "That would be monstrous."

"That's the first good idea you've had all day," said Penelope.

"I don't want to," said Suzie. "I don't like the dark."

"And ghost stories give me nightmares," said Poppy.

"That's the point of them," said Penelope. "And anyway, makeovers give me nightmares, so it's time for a little payback." She went over to the dimmer switch and turned the lights down. The others huddled in the middle of the room.

"We'd better put Violet away before it gets too dark," said Maud.

Poppy placed the dozing hamster back inside her cage. Then Penelope turned the lights down even further, so that they could barely make out each other's faces.

"Right," said Penelope. "Who wants to go first?"

"I do," said Milly. "Once upon a time, there was a family of ghosts, and they had a little ghost puppy who wanted to scare people but couldn't because he was too cute …"

Penelope let out a loud yawn. "Oh sorry," she said. "I thought we were telling scary stories. You must have misheard."

"I haven't finished yet," said Milly.

"Well, I don't think you should bother," said Penelope. "I've had Maths lessons more frightening than that. That's why I'm going to treat you all to one of my favourite stories, *The Haunted Doll*."

In the dim light, Maud could just about make out her sister. Milly was frowning, with her arms folded.

"Once upon a time," said Penelope, "there was an antique toy shop. Instead of selling shiny new toys, it sold ancient ones, like hobby horses with wide, crooked grins, and wooden dolls with sad, faded faces and button eyes …"

"I don't like this story," said Poppy, quivering slightly.

"No, I want to hear this so-called scary story," said Milly.

"Anyway," said Penelope, "after dark all the toys would come alive and creep around. You wouldn't want to be stuck in there at night …"

The Primrose Towers girls had huddled closer. Even Milly had unfolded her arms and was staring intently at Penelope.

Maud heard a faint rustling noise in the corner of the room. She turned and saw a tiny figure scraping across the floor towards them, with its thin legs moving in stiff strides.

The figure came into the circle of dim light in the middle of the room. It was one of Milly's old Barbie dolls.

Poppy, Alice and Suzie screamed, and Maud couldn't help but grin. She recognised Isabel's laughter, too. The Primrose Towers girls all fled to the door.

"Help!" sobbed Poppy.

"Make it go away!" begged Suzie.

Milly switched on the lights, and the doll lay still on the carpet.

"Penelope was just playing a trick," said Maud. "You're so easy to fool!"

Poppy stopped snivelling, and Alice passed

her a handkerchief.

"Uh-oh," said Paprika.

"Don't tell me you found the story too frightening as well?" said Maud.

"No," said Paprika. "I was looking over there."

He pointed at Violet's cage in the corner of the room. A trail of tiny flecks of red nail varnish led from it to the open bedroom door.

"Has anyone been messing around with that cage?" asked Maud.

"How could we?" asked Milly. "We were sitting right here listening to that horrid story."

"I'm sure I locked the door," said Poppy. "It looks like the catch has been broken."

Maud glanced at Penelope and noticed that she was looking at her feet and desperately trying not to giggle.

"Can I talk to you? In private?" Maud said.

She led Penelope and Paprika into the hallway and closed the door.

"Alright," she said, with her arms folded. "What's so funny?"

"I don't know what you mean," said Penelope, smirking.

"Yes, you do," said Maud. "You're up to something, and I'm going to find out what." She gave the witch a piercing look. "We're not really friends, so why did you come tonight?"

Penelope shrugged, a grin on her face.

"I just wanted to see how the pet-sitting was going. Violet's no ordinary hamster, you see. She's a vampster."

Paprika gasped.

"A vampster?" asked Maud.

"A vampire hamster," said Paprika. "My grandma told me about those. They were all the rage a hundred years ago, apparently. She said they were just as strong, cunning and mischievous as normal vampires. I didn't think monster pet shops sold them anymore."

"They don't," said Penelope. "Mr Quasimodo bought her online."

"There are loads of vampire animals," said Paprika. "We had a vampire dog once. It bit the postman, and we very nearly had to take it to the vet to get staked. Dear old Barkula."

"Good grief," said Maud. "We need to track down this vampster fast."

"We wouldn't be having all this trouble if you'd managed to hold on to this," said Penelope. She fished in the deep pocket of her black robes and pulled out a slip of torn notepaper, which she handed to Maud.

It was Mr Quasimodo's note.

"Why have you got this?" asked Maud. "Did you use a spell to blow it out of my hand?"

"Of course not," said Penelope, grinning again. "In fact, I was expecting you to be a little more grateful that I bothered to pick it up."

Maud looked down at Mr Quasimodo's note:

Care of Vampster
Important Instructions
DO NOT IGNORE

1. Do not place vampster in direct sunlight.

2. Do not overexcite vampster (avoid loud noises).

3. Do not bathe vampster in holy water.

4. Do not feed garlic to vampster (allergy).

5. Do not let vampster drink your blood, as this can lead to vampiric infection.

Maud tucked the sheet into her pocket. So it was Violet who'd been responsible for trashing the room and eating the pizza. Poor Quentin! No wonder he'd been so petrified all day! And now she'd imprisoned him in his cage for crimes he didn't commit. She'd have to give him an extra large helping of crisps tonight to make up for it all.

"You should have told us all this," said Maud to Penelope. "Just imagine if Violet had bitten Suzie. She might have turned her into a vampire, too. That would take some explaining."

"It was only a bit of fun," said Penelope.

"Well, you've had your fun," said Maud. "Now you can help me find Violet."

Maud followed the trail of nail varnish marks down the stairs. She put her finger to her lips and whispered, "Tracy said she doesn't want to be disturbed."

The tracks ran out halfway along the downstairs corridor, but it looked as though

Violet had been on her way to the kitchen.

Maud opened the kitchen door. The smell of garlic bread wafted to her nose. From the living room, she could hear the music of the horror film. Violet was nowhere to be seen.

"What's this?" asked Paprika. He pointed to a small wooden door opposite the staircase.

"The door to the cellar," said Maud. "We never really use it though."

"So why is it open, then?" asked Paprika.

Maud swallowed. He was right – the door was a couple of centimetres ajar.

"We'd better check down there," she said. "Who wants to go first?"

"I'd have thought a fearless monster like you would jump at the chance," said Penelope.

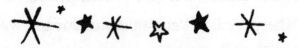

"Fine," said Maud. She grabbed her dad's torch from the shelf and flicked the switch.

A dim beam of light shone into the darkness.

Maud crept down the steps, which creaked beneath her feet. She cast the torch around, waiting for a flash of purple eyes. A thick layer of dust coated the shelves, and cobwebs hung around the boiler tank and between exposed pipes.

Maud shone the torch on something in the corner that looked like a grinning monster, then saw it was just an old pantomime horse her mum had sewn.

"Here, Violet!" called Maud.

A scuttling noise in the far corner made Maud swing the torch around. The beam caught a moving shadow – a round body and two grasping paws. Then it vanished.

"She's definitely here ..." said Maud.

"There!" cried Penelope, pointing.

Maud shone the torch and saw Violet squatting on top of a cardboard box and staring at them, her purple eyes glowing.

"Here, girl," said Maud.

Maud inched forwards and reached out as slowly and carefully as she could. She was just about to grab Violet, when a pair of leathery black wings flapped out from the vampster's back. Maud gasped and shrank back.

Violet fluttered her wings a few times before extending them fully, making her look like a fluffy, overweight bat. She leapt off the box, letting out a series of high-pitched chirps as she flew around the cellar.

"Catch her!" shouted Maud, pointing her torch at the airborne hamster.

Penelope and Paprika ran down the steps to try and seize her. Unfortunately, Paprika tripped over his cape and fell on to Penelope, who flew headfirst into a pile of old books. They crashed on to the floor, filling the cellar with a huge cloud of dust.

Maud ran in circles, sweeping the torch beam around and snatching through the dust with her free hand.

"Up there!" said Paprika. He pointed to the top of the stairs, just as the vampster flew through the open door into the kitchen.

Violet was on the loose!

Chapter Seven

Maud dashed back into the kitchen. One of the cupboard doors was swinging open, but there was no sign of Violet.

"Look at this," said Penelope, picking up an empty tin of tuna from the floor. "She must be strong to open this with her bare paws."

"She probably used her fangs as a can-opener," said Paprika. "Mum does that on long car journeys."

A wail rang out from the living room.

"Tracy!" shouted Maud.

She raced to the living room and flung open

the door. Inside, there was darkness except for the TV screen. In the glow of the flickering light cast by the horror movie, Maud saw Tracy cowering behind a pillow on the couch, with her eyes squeezed shut.

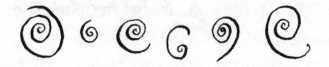

Paprika flicked on the light switch, and Tracy opened her eyes. She grabbed the remote and muted the TV, cutting out the shrieks and chainsaw noises.

"What are you lot up to now?" she asked.

"We heard screams," said Maud. "We thought …"

"Of course you heard screams," Tracy said. "I'm watching a horror film. Right, I've had enough. I'm ringing your parents right now!"

She leaned over, lifted up the phone receiver and jabbed at the keypad.

"Hello? Hello?" she asked, before reaching

around the back and lifting up the cord.

Maud gasped. The cable had been chewed right through. Then she saw a white shape scurrying beside the dresser on the far wall.

"Behind you!" she said, pointing past Tracy.

"Nice try," said Tracy, fumbling for her mobile. "I'm not falling for that one."

"No really," said Paprika. "Look behind you."

Violet crouched on the dresser, fanned out her black batwings behind her and rose up into the air. Then she swooped down on Tracy, snatching the mobile phone in her paws.

Tracy's mouth dropped open so wide that her chewing gum fell out. Above her, Violet glided back and forth, clutching the phone.

"Move over to the door," said Maud. "And don't scream. Vampsters go mad if they ..."

Tracy screamed.

"Oh dear," said Maud.

Violet dropped the phone and gave a shrill squeak. Her jaws opened wide and she bared her tiny fangs as she flew over Tracy's head.

"Get it off me!" shouted Tracy.

The door opened, and a piece of garlic bread hovered through the room towards Violet. The vampster let out a squeal of terror and backed away, flapping frantically.

"Good thinking, Isabel," murmured Maud.

"Thanks," said Isabel's voice.

Tracy pointed up at Violet, who was thrashing around near the ceiling. The vampster hit the lampshade with her left wing, and it swung back and forth, throwing light and shadow around the room.

"What ... What is ... that thing?" Tracy's eyes rolled back, and she fainted on to the couch.

✳ ★ ✳ ☆ ★ ✳

Violet hurled herself around the room faster and faster, knocking over books, sewing baskets and stacks of classic car magazines. She swept a glass of water to the floor, and it smashed into hundreds of pieces. Then she slammed headfirst into the TV, which wobbled forwards and backwards. Before Maud could reach it, it toppled over on to the carpet.

"Oh no!" said Maud. "Someone stop her!"

Paprika leapt for Violet and missed. The vampster flapped around in a mad blur, careering into one of the curtains. Her claws hooked into the material and ripped it down from the rails, one hook at a time. The curtain fabric fell over her, but underneath it Violet managed to keep flying. She shot towards the door. Maud grabbed hold of the other end of the curtain as she zipped past. It was like trying to stop a speeding truck. The vampster dragged her all the way down the hall and into the kitchen.

"I can't hold on much longer!" wailed Maud, straining to stop the vampster from shooting off.

"I've got an idea," said Isabel's voice from the far end of the kitchen. "Let go after three. One … two … three!"

Maud released her grasp, sending Violet hurtling towards the door at the back of the kitchen that led to the garage. Isabel flung the door open just long enough for the curtain-coated vampster to fly through, then slammed it shut.

"Excellent," said Maud, throwing herself against the door. "We've got her trapped now."

"Okay, let's think this through," said Maud. She was pressed up against the door at the back of the kitchen, next to Penelope and Paprika. "The three of us …"

"The four of us …" said Isabel.

"Sorry," said Maud. "The *four* of us have to deal with this before Mum and Dad get home."

She couldn't even *think* what to do about all the mess.

There was a violent thump on the other side of the door, which almost knocked her off her feet.

"Do you think she'll break it down?" asked Maud.

"Probably," said Paprika, his back against the door. "I've heard that vampsters are just as strong as any other type of vampire."

Another thud on the other side of the door sent Paprika sprawling.

"What's going on?" shouted Tracy from the living room.

"She's getting on my nerves," said Penelope. "Hold on. I'm going to cast a sleeping spell on her." She rushed out of the room.

Maud heard Penelope chanting, followed by loud snoring from the babysitter.

"Could you cast a spell like that on Violet?" asked Maud, as Penelope sprinted back in.

"Maybe," said Penelope. "I've never tried it on a vampster before. I practised on my black cat once, but he's so lazy it was hard to tell if it worked. Maybe if I got really close to her …"

"We could tempt her with another can of tuna," said Paprika. "She obviously loves it."

Milly flung open the kitchen door. "What's going on?" she asked. "We're trying to make friendship bracelets upstairs and we can't hear ourselves think."

There was another loud crash on the other side of the door.

"Nothing," said Maud. "Just a game."

"I'm telling Tracy," said Milly. She stomped off, creaked open the living-room door and let out a loud gasp. She ran back into the kitchen, her eyes widening. "You're going to be in soooo much trouble," she said.

✳ ✦ ✳ ✩ ★ ✳

Maud tried to think of a convincing explanation for all the destruction, but her mind was so frazzled after running around after Violet that she couldn't come up with anything. Plus, she would need all the help she could get if she was going to catch the vampster. Maybe it would be simpler if she told Milly what was really going on.

"I think it's about time I came clean," whispered Maud, taking Milly to one side. "You remember when I told you that Rotwood was a frightful place? Well, I meant it literally. It's not a school for human children at all. It's a school for monsters."

Milly snorted. "Very funny, I don't think."

"The hamster you're calling 'Cuddles' is actually a vampster, which is a cross between a normal hamster and a vampire. She was the one who caused all this damage, not us. We've just trapped her in the garage and we're trying to work out what to do. Paprika's a vampire, and Penelope's a witch."

"And I'm invisible," said Isabel.

"Whatever, Maud," said Milly. "You'll need to come up with a better story than that before Mum and Dad get home."

"I'm not lying," said Maud. "There's a monster behind that garage door, and you need to stop making silly friendship bracelets and help us!"

"There's only one monster behind that door," said Milly, "and that's your nasty pet rat."

"Quentin?" asked Maud. "I thought he was on my bed."

"No," said Milly. "He was grossing Suzie out with his horrible straggly fur, so she put him back in the garage where he belongs."

"Why did you let her do that?" asked Maud. "Now Violet's going to get him!"

Milly patted Maud on the head as if she was a dog. "Of course she is," she said. "I'm going back upstairs now. If you weirdos must play your silly monster game, keep the noise down."

Milly barged out of the kitchen and slammed the door.

"She was helpful," said Penelope. "Would you like me to cast a spell on her?"

"Maybe later," said Maud. "It's Violet we need to worry about now. Quentin's in danger!"

She grabbed a can of tuna and whirred it around her mum's automatic can-opener.

"Okay," she said, clutching the handle of the door. "Here goes ..."

Maud threw the door wide open, holding the can of tuna in front of her like a weapon.

In the pale moonlight cast by the high windows, she saw that the tools had been ripped down from the wall, leaving nothing but rusty pegs and painted outlines. All the nails and screws had been tipped out of her dad's toolbox into a chaotic pile on the floor. Poor Dad – he'd prided himself on how well ordered they were.

Maud tiptoed into the garage, followed by Penelope and Paprika, looking for signs of movement behind the scattered hammers and wrenches. She lifted up the living-room curtain, which had been dumped near the window on the other side of the garage, but Violet wasn't under it.

Maud scanned the room. "Where's Quentin's cage?"

"Uh-oh," said Paprika, pointing up. Maud saw that one of the windows was wide open. There were scratches around the frame. "This isn't good," he said. "This isn't good at all."

"Poor Quentin," said Maud. "Violet must have taken him!"

"Maybe she wants him to be her boyfriend," said Paprika. "She did seem pretty fond of him when they were in the wedding car. Though I don't think he felt the same."

"We've got to save him!" cried Maud.

"Have you seen this?" asked Isabel.

A flyer for the *Dracula* production floated up off the floor. It showed the Count with his fangs bared, about to sink them into the neck of a young woman in a nightie. It was covered in scratch marks, just like the ones on the window frame.

"Do you think vampsters can read?" Isabel asked.

"I don't know," said Paprika. "They are supposed to be very clever ..."

"Imagine all the havoc Violet could wreak if she went to the theatre," said Penelope, grinning again.

"This is serious," said Paprika. "We need to stop her."

"But I promised Mum that I wouldn't leave the house under any circumstances," said Maud.

"I'm sure she'll make an exception for this," said Paprika. "If Violet attacks the audience of your mum's play, imagine how bad the reviews will be!"

"You're right," said Maud. "Mum had no way of knowing there would be a supernatural pet on the loose when she made that rule. Let's go."

Chapter Eight

Maud frowned, thinking hard.

"The theatre's a couple of miles away," she said. "We can make it in half an hour if we run."

"That will be too late," said Penelope. "Violet's flying there right now. You won't catch up on foot."

"I can fly," said Paprika. "I could get there in no time."

"I've stashed my broomstick in the front garden," said Penelope. "So it won't be a problem for me either."

"Well, that settles it," said Maud. "I'll get a lift with you."

"No, you won't," said Penelope. "I'm not making that mistake again. Last time, you made me crash."

"You should have been looking where you were going," said Maud.

"Don't forget I need a lift, too," said Isabel. "I can't fly either, in case you hadn't noticed."

"Well, you can perch on my broom," said Penelope. "Maud, you'll just have to work it out for yourself."

"But I need to rescue Quentin," said Maud. "You can't leave me behind!"

"Fine," said Penelope. She snatched a mop from the corner of the garage and placed it on the floor. Then she held her hands over it and muttered under her breath.

The mop sprang up into the air and gave a clunk.

"Ouch," said Isabel. "That was my elbow."

Maud reached out and grabbed the levitating mop. It hummed gently beneath her fingers.

"This is safe, isn't it?" she asked. "It had better not run out of magic as soon as I'm up in the air."

"I might not like you," said Penelope, "but even I don't want you to end up splatted."

"Alright, then," said Maud. She opened the front door of the garage, guided the mop outside, then climbed on.

. ✶ ★ ✩ ✳ ✦ ✳

"How do I get it started?" she asked, gripping on to the front tightly.

Penelope sighed. "Point it up at the sky. Obviously."

Next to her, Paprika had closed his eyes and was clenching his fists tightly. He opened one eye. "Turn around. I can't do it when you're all watching."

Maud looked away, heard a puff, and turned back to see a cloud of smoke where Paprika had been standing. As it cleared, she saw a black bat hovering in the air.

Maud lifted up the front of her mop, but nothing seemed to be happening. "I don't think it's work—"

The mop shot up into the night sky, and Maud felt cold wind blasting against her skin. She wanted to close her eyes, but that would be far too dangerous. She needed to learn how to control it.

Maud steered right to avoid hitting an oak tree, only to find herself on course to crunch into a telegraph pole. She swung the front of the mop left so sharply that she span around in a circle.

"We don't have time for showing off," shouted Penelope.

Maud pushed the end of her mop down so it was pointing straight ahead. She leaned closer

to it and sped smoothly forward until she was
level with Penelope.

Maud could see rows of shining streetlights
below, spreading out like cobwebs around the
bright office blocks of the town centre. In the
distance, she saw a small shape flit past one of
the streetlights. As she peered at it, she could
just about make out the outline of a metal cage
and a flapping pair of wings above it.

"There they are!" shouted Maud.

The shape turned to look at them, and Maud
caught a flash of the vampster's bright purple
eyes.

Penelope leaned forward on her broomstick
and shot off in pursuit. Maud followed. They
gained on Violet and drew up on either side
of her. From inside the cage, Maud could hear
Quentin squeaking with terror.

"Cast your spell!" Maud called across to Penelope. "Quick!"

Penelope drew back her hands and recited the spell under her breath. She threw her arms forward, but at the last minute, Violet plunged rapidly down.

"Missed!" shouted Penelope.

"Drat!" said Maud.

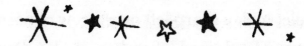

Violet plummeted like a diving seabird, and Maud tipped the mop into a steep descent. She hurtled to the ground, terrified that she would crash but determined to catch the vampster. She waited until she was down below the streetlights and then tugged the end of the mop up with all her strength. She hurtled along the pavement, as close to the ground as if she was riding a bike. Takeaways and minimarkets swooshed past on either side, as she sped down the road to the town centre.

Violet dropped so low that Quentin's cage scraped along the pavement. Maud followed, shooting through the sparks.

The vampster glanced back for a second and then swung out into the road. Maud followed, swerving around a car to keep up. As she passed, she glimpsed a young girl pointing at them from the back window.

Violet took a sharp left over a row of narrow gardens. Maud sped after her as she dipped under washing lines and over fences. In one of the gardens, a little dog jumped up and snapped at Quentin's cage, missing it by inches.

"Don't worry, Quentin," shouted Maud. "We're coming!"

When she got to the last garden in the row, Violet veered right into an alleyway with brick walls on each side. The wind whistled past Maud's ears as she swerved around dustbins and over an abandoned shopping trolley.

At the end of the alley, Violet swooped over a tree. As she shot past the branches, one caught on Quentin's cage and whipped open the hatch.

In the orange glow of a streetlight, Maud saw Quentin slip through the hanging cage door. Maud's scream caught in her throat, as Quentin dangled from the cage mesh by his claws. Then he was falling through the air, his legs flailing.

Maud steered firmly towards him and lifted her arms up, catching him just as he was about to crash into a postbox. She clasped him tightly to her chest, but as she let go of the mop, it swung round and round in the air. Maud reached out to grab the handle again, as the streetlights swam around her.

"Watch out!" shouted Penelope.

But Maud's spinning mop smashed into the witch's broom, and they both fell down to the pavement below. Maud landed in a pile of bin-bags outside a Chinese restaurant. She flicked a prawn cracker off her sleeve, and Quentin leapt into the front pocket of her cardigan and burrowed as deep as he could.

"You're safe now," said Maud.

Penelope was pulling a stale noodle out of her hair.

"Where's Isabel?" Maud asked. "Is she alright?"

"I'm fine," said a voice behind her. Maud looked around and saw a girl-shaped dent in one of the rubbish bags.

"We lost Violet," said Penelope.

A dark shape fluttered towards them and burst into a puff of smoke. Paprika fell on to the pavement face-first, then rolled on to his back.

"This is Wing's Chinese," said Isabel. "It's only a couple of streets away from the theatre.

We can catch her if we run."

Maud helped Paprika to his feet, and together they all raced along the pavement, passing newsagents and kebab shops until they reached a square surrounded by restaurants and bars. They dashed through the middle, dodging around a hotdog van that was just opening up for the night.

On the far side of the square stood the theatre, with two huge posters of Count Dracula draped across the front. A flight of wide steps led up to the entrance doors. As Maud got closer, she could see a small white shape hopping up them.

"Violet!" said Maud. "We're just in time."

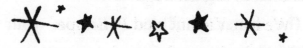

"Sorry. No late admissions," said the usher, stepping out to block their path.

"We really need to get in," said Maud. She peered around the usher to glance at the theatre foyer. Violet should have been easy to spot against the plush red carpet under the bright light of the chandeliers, but Maud couldn't see her. She must have got in without the usher noticing.

"I'm sure you can wait until the interval," said the usher. "It's only ten minutes away."

"But we need to go in now," said Isabel.

"Who said that?" asked the usher. He took a pair of glasses out of his pocket and put them on. "Where are your tickets, anyway?"

"We don't have any," said Maud. "But you'll have to take our word for it. If you don't let us in, you could be dealing with the biggest disaster ever seen in regional theatre."

The usher chuckled. "Be on your way, kiddies."

They trudged back down the steps.

"What an annoying man," said Penelope. "Would you like me to cast a fear spell on him? He'll be too busy screaming to notice us slip in."

"That sounds a bit horrible," said Maud. "Let's look for another way in."

"At least Isabel will have sneaked past," said Paprika. "That's something."

"Er … actually I didn't think of that," said Isabel's voice beside him. "Sorry."

"Great," said Penelope. "What's the point of being invisible if you don't use it when we really need it?"

"I didn't ask to be invisible," said Isabel, crossly. "Sometimes I wish my mum had married a human. Then at least I'd be visible from the waist up like my cousin Clarabel."

"I can see a stage door round the side," said Maud. "Let's try that."

They crept around the edge of the building. The usher standing in front of this one was a skinny teenager with floppy brown hair and a

waistcoat that was far too big for him.

He held his hand out to stop them. "If you're after autographs, you'll have to wait. They haven't even got to the interval yet."

"We don't want autographs," said Penelope. "We need to come inside. You see, there's this creature that's a cross between a hamster and a ..."

"What she means to say," said Paprika, "is that I'm the understudy for Dracula in tonight's performance, and I'm needed backstage."

Paprika held out his cape and pointed at his fangs.

"Aren't you a little short to be an understudy?" asked the usher.

"All actors are shorter in real life," said Paprika.

The usher narrowed his eyes. "And who are the others?"

"I'm his agent," said Maud.

"And I'm make-up," said Penelope.

"And I'm …" began Isabel, but Maud quickly coughed to drown out her voice.

The usher paused a few seconds, then moved out of the way. "In you go, then."

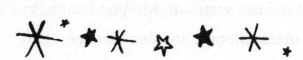

Maud followed Paprika and Penelope into the corridor. Unlike the foyer with its bright lights and deep red carpets, this side of the theatre was cramped and dim, with bare brick walls and a dusty floor.

The end of the corridor led straight to the side of the stage, where spooky piano music was playing, faster and faster. Maud stepped carefully over the cables on the floor and glanced out across the stage.

A dry-ice machine was pumping thick smoke across a graveyard set, as Miss Bloom tiptoed across the stage, looking scared. A shadow rose from the rolling mist – a man wearing a black cape. He crept up behind Miss Bloom, reaching out with long fingers.

"That's your dad!" hissed Maud, gripping Paprika's arm.

At the last moment, Mr Von Bat backed away from Miss Bloom. She ran off stage.

Penelope turned to Paprika and whispered, "Did you know your dad was in this play?"

"No," said Paprika. "I thought my parents were at the Archduke of Prussia's ball tonight."

Quentin poked his head out of Maud's pocket and peeked at the scene.

Then he squeaked with fear and ducked down again.

"It's alright," whispered Maud. "It's just a play, and he's not a real vampire, anyway."

In fact, she was telling Quentin the truth. Everyone at Rotwood School thought that Paprika's dad was a real vampire. But Maud knew that he was really just a human pretending to be a vampire.

As the first half of the play built to its climax, Mr Von Bat lay down in a coffin that appeared on the stage. Another blast of smoke swept across the graveyard set, and the heavy red curtain was lowered to the sound of loud applause.

Maud glanced over her shoulder and saw her mum was coming down the corridor. Thankfully, she hadn't spotted them yet.

"Quick," Maud said. "We need to hide somewhere!"

"Down here," said Paprika. He led Maud, Isabel and Penelope down a flight of steps to a cramped space under the stage.

At the end of the room, ropes creaked around metal pulleys, and the coffin sank down from the stage. There was nowhere to run. Ahead of them was the coffin with Mr Von Bat, and behind them, Mrs Montague. As stray swirls of dry ice swept across the coffin, the lid creaked open. Mr Von Bat sprang up, his pale face emerging from the shadows.

"Dear, oh dear," he muttered, rubbing his back. "I'm too old for this!"

He looked up and saw Maud, Penelope and Paprika. His eyes narrowed. "Either I'm going mad," he said, "or someone needs to explain what is going on. Right now."

Chapter Nine

Maud stood in Mr Von Bat's small dressing room.

"So you see, we need to find Mr Quasimodo's hamster," she said. "Except that she's not a hamster at all. She's a vampster. And she's loose in the theatre."

Maud leaned against the wardrobe, while Mr Von Bat fixed his make-up in the mirror. Penelope and Paprika were sitting on a costume chest.

"I had my suspicions about that creature," said Mr Von Bat. "Mr Quasimodo likes to keep some very strange pets. He had a baby dragon once, but the Head made him get rid of it when it burned down the broom shed. Why did you bring such a dangerous creature here?"

"We didn't bring her!" said Maud. "She read a leaflet about it and flew here."

"Only after Maud left her on her own in the garage," said Penelope.

"Penelope knew about Violet all along," said Maud.

"I'm not interested in whose fault it was," said Mr Von Bat. "The fact is we've got a serious problem. You know how hard the Head works to keep Rotwood a secret from all the humans in this town? All that could be undone in seconds if the audience sees you all chasing around after a flying fanged hamster."

Brisk footsteps echoed down the corridor outside.

"I recognise the sound of those high heels," said Paprika. His skin was even paler than usual, and his hands were trembling. "It's Mum!"

Maud gulped. Penelope swallowed. If Isabel reacted, no one could see. Mrs Von Bat was a genuine vampire, and even Mr Von Bat was frightened of her.

"Get in the wardrobe," said their teacher. "Hurry!"

Maud, Paprika and Penelope clambered into the dusty wooden cupboard.

"Your elbow is squashed in my face," whispered Penelope.

"Sorry," said Maud. "But it's got nowhere else to go."

"What about that massive empty space next to you?" asked Penelope.

"It's not empty," said Isabel. "I'm here."

"What are you doing in here, you idiot?" hissed Penelope.

"You don't need to hide!"

"Sorry," said Isabel. "I didn't want to be left out."

Through a small keyhole, Maud could make out Mr Von Bat cowering in front of his dressing table, while his wife stood over him with her arms folded.

"The scene in the dining room was adequate," she said. "But the less said about the rest, the better. As for the blood-drinking, it was quite the worst I've ever seen. And I've seen a lot."

"Oh," said Mr Von Bat. "I thought the audience was rather enjoying it."

"Nonsense," said Mrs Von Bat. "They were bored to tears. And I didn't like the way that young Miss Bloom was looking at you either."

"She was only acting, dear."

"A likely story."

A feather from a boa at the top of the wardrobe floated down next to Maud's nose. She held her breath, desperate to avoid sneezing.

"ACHOO!" A loud sneeze rang out next to Maud. "Sorry," said Isabel.

Through the keyhole, Maud saw Mrs Von Bat turn to look at the cupboard. "What was that?" she asked.

She stepped over to the wardrobe, her high heels clacking on the floor, and reached out for the handle.

Behind her, the door swung open, and Maud's mum appeared, carrying a clipboard.

"Places for Act Two," she said, and darted off.

Mrs Von Bat turned away from the cupboard and strutted over to the door. "You'd better improve your performance in the second half," she said. "Don't let me down."

When she'd gone, Mr Von Bat opened the wardrobe door, and they all piled out again, gasping for air.

"Right," said Mr Von Bat. "You need to find the creature and keep it away from the audience. I need to be back on stage. My public awaits."

With a swirl of his cape, Mr Von Bat straightened his fangs and strode out.

"Three of us have got no chance against that flying monster!" said Penelope.

"The four of us," said Maud. "Isn't that right, Isabel?"

There was no reply.

"I think she's gone," said Paprika. "She got upset when Penelope called her an idiot."

"Well, we don't have time to look for her now," said Maud. "We need to find that vampster before it ruins my mum's show."

They walked out into the corridor, this time taking a right turn down a passageway that led directly behind the stage. Maud could hear the piano tinkling away again, announcing the start of the second half.

Paprika held his hand up to stop them.

"Can you hear that?"

"What?" asked Maud.

"Squeaking," said Paprika.

"It's probably just Maud's wimpy rat," said Penelope.

Maud checked inside her pocket and saw Quentin staring up at her with his wide black eyes. He certainly looked frightened, but he wasn't making a sound.

Maud stepped over to a set of double doors leading off the passageway. Paprika was right. There was a shrill squeaking coming from the other side.

Maud swung the doors open to reveal a large kitchen lit by a flickering striplight. A horde of mice skittered out, squealing in fright.

Maud ventured inside. There was a small white fridge in the corner with its door swinging open. A yoghurt pot, a pint of milk and an empty ham packet were scattered underneath.

"It doesn't look as if she found much in

there," said Paprika. "She'll still be hungry."

They passed through the door at the back of the kitchen and emerged into another murky corridor.

"There!" shouted Paprika.

At the end of the corridor, Maud saw a small white shape flit into a room marked **PROPS**.

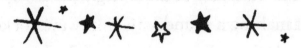

Maud rushed into the room after Violet and flicked on the light switch. Nothing happened. She tried it again, but the room remained dark.

"Guard the door," said Maud to Penelope. "Grab her if she flies past."

Penelope nodded.

As her eyes adjusted to the gloom, Maud could make out rows of pirate hats, genies' lamps and wooden swords. She noticed a closed cupboard in the corner of the room. She put one finger to her lips and pointed with the other.

Paprika nodded.

Together they edged towards the wardrobe.

"Get ready to catch her if she leaps out," Maud murmured.

Paprika grabbed a butterfly net from one of the shelves and held it in front of the cupboard. Maud inched open the first door, expecting to be greeted by a pair of unblinking purple eyes.

A huge brown shape with empty eye sockets leapt out at her.

Maud screamed and threw it to the ground. But as she glanced down, she saw the object was just a crumpled bear costume.

Maud opened the second door, revealing a grinning plastic skull.

"It looks like Bartholomew Bones from 2C," said Paprika.

"All the Bones brothers look the same to me," muttered Penelope.

Maud crept around the room, looking under plastic crates and lifting up costumes.

"I don't understand where she could have gone," said Maud. "You didn't let her escape, did you?"

"Of course not," said Penelope. "You just need to look harder."

Maud turned back to Paprika in time to see something flat and slimy fall down on to his shoulder.

"What is it?" he yelped. "Get it off me!"

"It's a slice of ham," said Maud.

"Uh-oh," said Paprika, pointing above their heads.

Maud looked up and saw Violet hanging from a loose ceiling panel. She was chewing another of the ham slices and staring at them. Suddenly, her glowing eyes turned from purple to red, and she dropped towards Maud.

Maud swung her arms up to try and catch

the plummeting vampster, but the furry fiend swerved out of the way.

"Grab her!" shouted Maud.

"I'm trying," said Paprika, swinging his butterfly net around and knocking hats and swords off the shelves.

Penelope rushed over from the doorway and flailed around in the darkness.

"I've found her!" she shouted.

A squeak of pain rang out from Maud's pocket.

"That's Quentin," said Maud. "Stop squeezing him!"

Just then, Maud spotted Violet's red eyes glaring at her from a shelf at the side of the room. She lunged forward, but at the same moment, Paprika's butterfly net swished down on to her head, sending her crashing to the floor.

"I've got her," said Paprika.

"That's me!" shouted Maud.

Penelope reached for Violet, but she tripped

over Maud and landed on top of her.

Maud scrambled free and got back to her feet, only to see Violet's silhouette flapping out of the door.

By the time Maud had raced back into the kitchen, the vampster was swooping around the corner. Maud darted after her and found herself back in the corridor that led down to the side of the stage. Mr Von Bat was standing at the end, smoothing down his shirt and taking deep breaths.

"Watch out, Sir!" shouted Maud.

※ ✶ ✳ ☆ ★ ※

Mr Von Bat gaped as Violet whooshed down the corridor towards him. He tried to cower away from her but she dug her claws into his collar. The teacher screamed as his toes left the ground, and the vampster dragged him out on to the stage.

Maud ran after them, leaping over the power cables on the floor. Behind her, Paprika tripped over one of them and fell flat on his face. There was a loud fizzing noise and a fountain of sparks from the cable, then the lights in the corridor and in the auditorium went out.

"Oops!" said Paprika.

Maud leapt out on to the side of the stage. Miss Bloom was lying on a bed in a nightdress, looking confused. The only light still working was a bright spotlight, which was fixed on Mr Von Bat as he writhed around under Violet's grip, with his arms and legs flapping wildly.

Violet flew up into the air, lifting Mr Von Bat over the coffin and up above the audience. The crowd gasped, as he floated above them, trying to struggle free of Violet.

On stage, Miss Bloom sat up on the bed, craning her neck to follow Mr Von Bat as he swirled over the auditorium. "I'm sure this isn't in the script," she said.

Mr Von Bat kicked his legs so violently that one of his shoes dropped off and fell on to the lap of a woman wearing a green dress, who leapt out of her seat. Maud could see several other audience members shuffling around uncomfortably now.

"We've got to do something," said Maud. "Mum will be so upset. Could you try casting the sleeping spell, Penelope?"

"Not really," said Penelope. "It's a bit hard to control. What if I send the audience to sleep instead? I don't think the cast would be very happy about that."

Violet swooped back towards the front of the auditorium, still carrying the squirming body of Mr Von Bat. This was a disaster! But just as the vampster reached the stage, the huge red safety curtain came crashing down, curtain rings and all, dragging her to the stage with a mighty crash. The audience could still see everything on stage, but at least the vampster was trapped.

For a moment, everyone was silent with shock. Then Mr Von Bat crawled out from under the heavy fabric, rubbing his head. The curtain material lurched up and down as the vampster tried to free herself.

Suddenly, Maud had an idea. "Quick," she hissed to Paprika, "set off the smoke machine." Then she turned to Penelope and said, "Open the coffin and get ready!"

Paprika flicked the switch on the small black box at the side of the stage, and dry ice flooded out.

Maud sneaked through the thickening fog to the fold under which Violet was straining. She lifted it up carefully and the vampster flapped out in a daze. Straight away, Maud grabbed her by the wings and shoved her into the open coffin.

Penelope slammed the lid shut and sat on it beside Maud. The coffin rattled as it sank beneath the stage, taking them with it.

As they descended through the billowing fog to the cramped room beneath, the spotlight above them went out at last, and the theatre erupted into loud applause.

Chapter Ten

aprika came pounding down the stairs. "Hop on!" said Maud.

Paprika plonked himself down between the girls. Underneath them, the coffin jerked back and forth as Violet tried to escape, squeaking at the top of her voice. It reminded Maud of the time her dad drove their car down a bumpy lane to show off the suspension, and made everyone travel sick.

Above the applause of the crowd, Maud heard someone else coming down the steps. She recognised the flat blue shoes, grey trousers and green blouse before she saw the person's face. It was her mum. Maud's heart sank.

"What are you lot doing here?" Mrs Montague asked, frowning at them from behind her big, round spectacles. "You weren't supposed to leave the house."

"It's perfectly fine," said Maud. "I can explain. We … er …"

Maud tried to come up with something that would convince her mum, but she couldn't think of anything. Perhaps she should just tell the truth.

"It's because Maud wanted to see your show," said Penelope. "She was really upset when she wasn't allowed to go because she was so proud of you and Mr Montague. She just knew you'd pull it off."

Maud looked over at Penelope in confusion. Was it possible that the witch was actually being nice to her?

"And just listen to the crowd," said Paprika.

"They loved it."

"Yes, I suppose they did," said Mrs Montague, a smile forming on her lips. But then she looked down at Maud and frowned again. "But it doesn't matter why you wanted to come. You still left the house without permission, and I'm very disappointed."

"Sorry," said Maud.

The cheering above them got even louder.

"Maybe you should go and take a bow," said Paprika. "It sounds like the crowd are demanding it."

"Well, I suppose … Oh very well," said Mrs Montague, clacking back up the steps. "But I'll deal with you later."

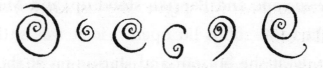

Maud sighed. "Thank goodness the curtain fell down. That's a stroke of luck," she said.

"Luck?" said a familiar voice beside them.

"Luck had nothing to do with it."

"Isabel!" said Maud. "Thanks for that."

"Maybe I'm not such an idiot after all," said Isabel.

"Yes, fine," said Penelope, grumpily. "I'm sorry, okay?"

Maud realised that the coffin wasn't moving any more.

"What should we do about you-know-who?" asked Paprika, nodding downwards.

"I'm not sure," said Maud. "She seems to have calmed down."

Maud stepped down from the coffin and put her ear to the side. All she heard was a gentle scratching. "I think it's safe," she said.

Penelope and Paprika stood up, and Maud inched the coffin lid open. Violet was sitting calmly at the bottom and staring up at them. Her eyes had returned from red to violet, and her wings were tucked back up into her fur. In fact, she looked pretty much as she'd done the day Mr Quasimodo first handed her over.

"I think she's gone tame again," said Maud. She scooped Violet up in her hands and examined her. Inside her pocket, she could feel Quentin trembling.

"It's alright, Quentin," said Maud. "I don't think she's going to ratnap you again."

"I'd keep an eye on her," said Paprika. "Just in case."

Maud held Violet carefully in front of her as she walked up the stairs between Paprika and Penelope. Isabel – invisibly – followed them.

They trundled back down the corridor, then found their way through a series of passages to the bright foyer.

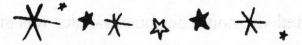

Mr Von Bat was in front of the concession stand, accepting a bunch of flowers from a young woman. His cheeks were flushing red, and he was beaming with pride as he greeted his fans.

Maud's mum and dad were over by the door, chatting to delighted members of the audience.

"The costumes were top notch," said a lady in a purple coat. "And the special effects were absolutely outstanding. I couldn't see the wires at all."

"The finale was better than anything we've ever seen in the West End," said a man in a tweed jacket. "How on earth did you pull it off?"

Mrs Montague smiled. "A good magician never reveals her secrets."

"Especially when she doesn't know them herself," muttered Paprika.

Over at the concession stand, Mrs Von Bat had come to join her husband and was glaring at the woman who'd given him the flowers.

"We'd better go before Mum sees me," said Paprika.

Maud nodded and went to tug on her mum's

sleeve. "It's late now," she said. "Perhaps we should get home."

Mr Montague led them all to his car, parked around the corner.

As they set off down the road, Maud noticed that Violet had dropped off to sleep in her cupped hands, and was snoring away happily. She was just about to breathe a sigh of relief, when her mum said, "It will be good to get back to a nice quiet house after all that."

"Drat," muttered Maud, under her breath. "I forgot about the house."

She thought about the awful destruction – the ripped curtains, the broken TV, the overturned furniture and the snoozing babysitter. It was no use. She'd have to come clean.

"I'm sure they'll understand," whispered Paprika.

"And I'm sure they won't," said Penelope, smirking. All her earlier niceness seemed to have disappeared.

Mr Montague parked outside their house, and they all climbed out of the car. As they walked up the garden path, Maud braced herself for the telling-off of her life.

As her dad put the key in the lock, Maud hung back. "Mum …" she began.

"Mm?" said Mrs Montague.

"I need to tell you something …"

But her parents were already stepping into the house. Maud waited for a scream, but none came. She followed them in, and her jaw dropped.

The living room was immaculate. The TV was back on its stand, the glass had been swept up, the curtain was neatly up on its rail, and the books were on their shelves again. Maud walked through the room with her mouth hanging open. She flicked through a pile of

Mr Montague's car magazines, and saw that they were even in date order, just as he liked them.

"Do you think Tracy did this?" asked Paprika.

"I doubt it," said Penelope. "Not when there's TV to be watched."

"Where is Tracy, anyway?" asked Maud. "I thought she'd still be snoozing on the couch."

✳ ✦ ✳ ☆ ★ ✳

"What on earth is the matter?" said Mr Montague from the hallway.

Maud rushed out and saw that her dad had found the babysitter whimpering in the cupboard under the stairs.

"There's a monster in this house," she sobbed. "It tried to attack me. It's … there it is!"

She pointed at the hamster snoozing peacefully in Maud's hands.

"Have you been watching horror films again?" asked Mrs Montague.

"No! Well, I mean, yes," said Tracy. "But this happened afterwards."

Mr Montague turned to Mrs Montague and shook his head. "The poor girl's rotted her brain."

"Thank you for babysitting, anyway," said Mrs Montague, taking a twenty-pound note out of her purse. But Tracy just yelped with fear and ran out of the front door, leaving Mrs Montague holding the note and looking very confused.

She pursed her lips and turned to Maud. "I'm still angry with you for leaving the house without permission, but it's very sweet that you wanted to share our moment of theatrical triumph. Now please go to bed."

Mr and Mrs Montague headed for the kitchen.

"Thanks for helping," Maud said to her friends.

"All three of you."

"Don't mention it," said Isabel.

"I guess it was sort of fun," said Penelope.

Paprika yawned. "I'm ready for bed."

Together, they crept upstairs to the bedroom.

On the pink half of the carpet, Milly and her Primrose Towers friends were fast asleep with their pyjamas and eye masks on.

Maybe Milly tidied up, thought Maud. If so, it was the nicest thing her sister had ever done for her. The only nice thing, in fact. But stranger things had happened. Even Penelope had been helpful earlier on.

Maud placed Violet carefully back into her cage and slotted it under the bed. Penelope, Isabel and Paprika settled into their sleeping bags on the floor.

"We'll have to get you a new cage tomorrow,"

she whispered to Quentin. "You can sleep on my pillow tonight."

Maud lay down on the bed, resting her head on the pillow. Quentin curled up next to her ear and thanked her with a sleepy squeak. He was obviously exhausted by his traumatic night, and Maud was feeling very tired, too.

Ouch! There was something hard underneath the pillow.

Maud sat up and pulled out the portrait of her great-aunt Ethel. Weird – she was sure she'd put it in her drawer. Perhaps Milly and her friends had been snooping?

Maud was about to put the picture back, when it tingled in her hand. She gasped and almost dropped it when her great-aunt gave her a wave from inside the frame.

"Wow," said Maud. "Was it you who tidied up?"

Great-aunt Ethel winked.

"Is that why you put the picture under my

pillow – to let me know?"

The ghost nodded.

"Monstrous!" said Maud. "Tidying up must have taken hours!"

She slipped out of bed to put the picture back in her drawer. "Thank you," she whispered to her great-aunt.

Maud stepped over her snoozing friends and got back into bed.

"Not bad for my first monster sleepover," she said to herself, as she drifted off to sleep.

Other titles by A. B. Saddlewick:

ISBN:
978-1-78055-072-5

ISBN:
978-1-78055-073-2

ISBN:
978-1-78055-075-6

EVEN MORE
Monstrous Maud
STORIES COMING SOON!

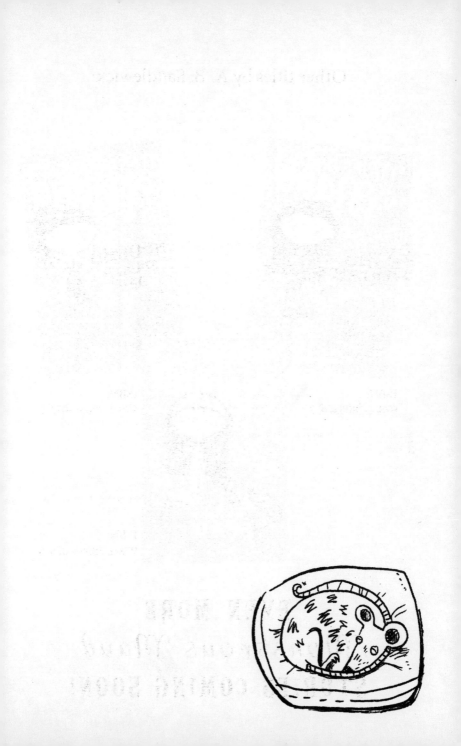